"You slept with my sister, Mr. Kendall."

He leaned forward, and the black threat on his face made Leigh draw back sharply.

"Yes, I did, Miss Walker. Two consenting adults. And if you're going to try and blackmail me, then you're barking up the wrong tree."

"I have no intention of blackmailing you, Mr. Kendall." Just what sort of world did this man move in, where blackmail featured on the menu? "I've come here to break some rather...unexpected news. I've come to tell you that you're a father. You have a seven-year-old daughter. Her name is Amy."

Dear Reader,

A perfect nanny can be tough to find, but once you've found her you'll love and treasure her forever. She's someone who'll not only look after the kids but also could be that loving mom they never knew. Or sometimes she's a he and is the daddy they are wishing for.

Here at Harlequin Presents® we've put together a compelling series, NANNY WANTED!, in which some of our most popular authors create nannies whose talents extend way beyond taking care of the children! Each story will excite and delight you and make you wonder how any family could be complete without a nineties nanny.

Remember—nanny knows best when it comes to falling in love!

The Editors

Look out next month for:

A Nanny for Christmas by Sara Craven (#1999)